YES DADDY

IT'S NOT A DADDY TALE

S. KAYSH

Made with ♥ on the Notion Press Platform
www.notionpress.com

Contents

Prologue

If you're fond of mystery and thrill books, then you picked correct one, YES DADDY is not actually sounds like it's title.

Rose, who was a 15 years old girl already facing problems in her life, Yes she wasn't ever a happy person of course life is so unfair. And as usual an incident changed her life forever as we all know our life takes turns and those are plot twists of our lives.

Rose, claimed that her mother's boyfriend Arthur who was all rounder complete man, killed her mother just to ate her property and that was her silly alligation. But as the story going on it takes place more interesting parts. So are you ready to start this journey with Rose? And ready to pulled down curtains from truth? Dark truths?

ONE
MEET ARTHUR

"Rose Come on we getting late dear" My mother called me from the threshold, I was staring in my dressing mirror cause my mood was spoilt, the reason was my mother, we're going to meet her one and only new boyfriend. Yes, it's true in the month of June she told me she has a boyfriend and she's serious this time, but I'm pretty sure this man is not the same person, he's someone else she met a month ago and she fell in love with him harder. Well, she does Everytime no doubt, when your mother looks like your elder sister, yes she's just 30 and I'm 15...

"Rose...." she shouted, I grabbed my bag from the bed and ran down, Taxi was at the gate we sat in and here we go again, I hate meeting her Boyfriends it's embarrassing I should introduce her as my Boyfriend not her, but I think I won't do it every in my life, I don't like dating things, maybe because I saw my mom or some other reason. Mom said she wasn't like this since Start, she was sincere and got pregnant at the age of 14 with me, what a sincere woman! Well, who cares? I have no right to judge her life but still, she's my mother, and people judge me through her character.

"Rose where you lost come on we arrived" I boarded from Taxi, it was a restaurant, of course, we entered.

She waved a hand over a man who was sitting on the corner table, wearing a grey suit with a red tie, perfectly combed hair partly on one side. Having a boxy jawline, oh it's sharp. Don't know from where mom found him? And why he's interested in my mother?

"Hi, I'm sorry we're late" she apologized, he pulled the chair for her, I managed myself before he stepped forward for me.

"So, let me introduce you first, she's my daughter Rose and Rose he's Arthur... Arthur Walker " she introduced us.

"It's nice to meet you Miss" he said in his ocean-deep voice.

"what's your age?" My stupid mind worked like this when I'm nervous.

"Rose" she pinched my hand under the table. He cackled.

"31... Don't worry I'm older than your mother" May he knew what my mind was thinking.

"She's silly ignore her stupid question" She tried to cover up.

"No that's fine, in fact I like it, straight to the point no?"

"Yes, I'm straight forward"

"Rose can you shut your mouth" she grinded her teeth.

"So, what do you like to eat Rose?"

"Nothing I'm full"

"Pasta, she likes pasta" again she jumped between.

"Fine, so we order pasta anything else you want?"

I pretend, I was busy by just scrolling my phone screen.

"Umm Rose... Actually we invited you here, cause we decided to take a step forward" she spoke politely.

"What? To the bed?" she glared.

"Your daughter is way too interesting" he was beaming.

"Better you behave now, Rose"

"Fine... Say"

"We decided to give more time to each other, we are familiar with our habits and all, but still we want to assure, and want you too to be part of our practice" I was confused.

"What... What are you saying?"

"Living... She's talking about a living relationship" I was too disappointed, not surprised but.

"Mom if you want, then go but please don't drag me into this"

"After marriage, we have to stay at his place, I just want you to be comfortable with him, with new neighbors"

"Mom please, I have school and friends, I don't want new ones..." I turned my face.

"Fine if she's not comfortable, then I'll shift to your place" I widened my eyes.

"Mr. Walker... How can you... No please"

"Rose, you promised me you'll stand by my side always, I gave you birth at a young age, and you...." She sobbed. Her emotional blackmailing, I'm so done.

"Fine... Whoever wants to stay, he can I won't change my room"

"I'm not even asking for... All I want is just to accept me"

I rolled my eyes, crossed my hands on my chest.

TWO DAYS LATER.

Arthur shifted at our place and that was totally discomfiting me. But I was helpless in front of my mother.

Someone knocked on the door.

"Yes, come in..." I thought it was mom, but it was Arthur.

"Mr. Walker..."

"Yes, Your room is pretty nice"

"Mr. Walker, better you don't come in my room again"

"You're still angry with Me?"

"Why do you want to marry my mom? Don't you have any other woman in your life? She's mother of a 15-year-old girl"

"Well, she looks like your sister tho"

"fine, she ages like a fine wine... But why you? Haven't you married yet?"

"No, I was busy establishing my business"

"So you're rich"

"Yes, not a millionaire but yes, I'm rich"

"Still no match, She's just an ordinary woman, and I see you having good looks too, then why she?"

"There's the reason behind"

"What?"

"None of your business... As you know, now I'm your Dad... So better you call me Daddy" his evil smirk.

"I'm sorry but you haven't married her yet"

"we will soon... But as you know this period is for practice, so we should start from today"

"No... I'll call you Mr. Walker" he sniffed.

"Look darling if I'm behaving well, you should behave good too, or else if I show my bad side you'll regret it for life" his brown eyes were staring at my soul.

"Dad... Sounds good"

"Daddy... Sounds better" He pinched my cheek. I swatted his hand.

He has bitten his lower thick lip.

"Take care... There's a lot of moments that remain to be real......"

I frowned.

Days passed like hours, don't know when Arthur became our family member and everyone accepted him too, society is too unfair when he's rich he can do anything and it's fair but if a girl like me did the same they'll be called me whore. There was a charm in Arthur that attracts everyone, and people were convinced by what he demanded. Or maybe he was manipulative.

"Rose, is your new dad home?"

"No, why?"

"Come on I know he's"

"I think you should focus on books more than my stepfather"

"he's hot... Handsome, tall, macho Ohh man he's perfect" Selena said, my close friend.

"I don't think so every man who has such qualities in him has a good heart"

"You sure? Who wants a man with good heart when he has a good bank balance?"

"you're so cheap..." she laughed like a monster.

"Rose..." my best friend cum neighbor, Alan called me. I turned myself.

"Alan..."

"Sup..."

"Good, you say"

"Finally you're here, I thought you won't going to join the school back"

"Why should I hide? When they're culprits"

"People will talk for some days but everything will be fine soon"

"some britches thinks, he's my Sugar Daddy" Selena laughed again.

"Sugarrrrr Daddddyyyyyy... Sounds perfect he suits you more than your mother" she teased me.

"I think that's why, They all think like this... Or maybe jealous" Alan tried to light my mood.

"Alan you too? Please for god sake...."

"Okay fine... Smile for me... Good girl" I fake smiled.

I arrived home after a long tiring day.

"Mom... Mom where are you?" I was panting, untie my shoe lace. Threw it aside.

"Your mom is not home honey" he walked out of kitchen, wearing an apron.

"what you doing in kitchen?"

"Cooking"

"Do you know cooking?"

"Yups"

"Hmmm... Where's mom?"

"She said she'll return home soon, she had some work remained at store"

"She told me she'll be home today"

"She'll be here soon love"

"First don't call me such names... My name is Rose"

"It's my choice what I want to call you"

"Then fine Mr Walker" he shook head while smiling on ground, all sudden his veiny hands grabbed my neck and pinned me with the wall.

"I'm not choking you but I can, better you call me Daddy next time sweetie... Hmm wasn't that deal?"

I nodded in low, he freed me, I was coughing.

"I didn't choke you, stop acting I'm doing domestic violence"

"You're a monster... I'll tell this mom"

"Sure what you gonna say... Daddy chocked me" his words always on point his double mean jokes, jerk.

"Fu...." I sighed and ran to my room.

"Food is ready, wash your hands and come down honey" he said it aloud.

I slammed door, I hate his dominating behavior, how ill manner person my mother choosen for rest of her life.

I was eating dinner, my mother poured wine in my glass.

"I don't drink mom... You know"

"yes, but you should start drinking... You can"

"If she's saying No, then why you forcing her?" He said. I drank wine all once, just to jealous him but vomited on my dress.

"Do you know Rose, you shouldn't do acts that doesn't suits you..." he cleaned my dress with a napkin.

"How lovely he is? And you say he's creepy?" I regret my life decision on time, why I even shared my thoughts with her?

"Creepy?" He again piercing my soul with his sharp eyes.

"Ummm mom, I'm done thank you."

I excused myself and came in my room, living among them was a trauma, I was facing humiliation and domestic violence same time, my mother wasn't ready to hear me cause all she could see was Arthur and why not? He was far good at her point. My mental health was all ill. I wanted to talked with a doctor, but my wallet was empty for paying the fee.

I took shower for going school, I was changing my clothes I heard someone knocked slow on door, I knew it was Arthur. So I made him wait on door, I opened the door.

"You like to tease me no?"

"I was changing"

"If you called me, I'll help you"

"No thanks, what?"

"Your mother going on trip with her colleague, so be on time 6 O'clock sharp"

"Why? Mom... Wait" I pushed him and rushed down, like it was last race of my life.

"Mom"I stopped her on threshold.

" Roooseeee" she gritted teeth.

"How many times I need to say don't call me when I'm leaving"

"Mom, you leaving me here alone with him?"

"what do you mean... Him? He's your father"

"not real"

"better than him"

"mom, take me with you"

"It's only night stay... It's a business trip not picnic so stay here"

"I'll take care of her, don't worry" he landed hand on my shoulder, I jolted my shoulder.

"Mom" I held her hand.

"Rose, act like your age girls....." She slammed door on my face, a tear dropped of my eye. He wiped it. I was broke don't know but staying with him alone was biggest nightmare of mine, I ran out of house to bus stop, while my tears falling through my jaw.

Entire day, I was thinking how I'm gonna deal with that monster who was already at home? I was drown in my deep thoughts, Selena scared Me.

"Selena... Oh my God" my hands were shivering.

"You okay?"

"No, I'm not... I'm totally lost... Mom went on trip and Arthur and I home alone"

"Woahhhh interesting"

"shut up... I'm dying here after thinking what will happen next and you"

"What? Is he doing wrong with you?"

"Selena stay at my place... Just for night please" I requested.

She was curious to meet Arthur so she was glad that I invited her at my place. She eaten my head entire way we returned home, asking about him.

"I don't know what he likes or not... Why don't you just ask him... We're near"

We arrived home, I rang the bell, Alan met us.

"Hey, Selena are you staying here?"

"Yups with her hot step dad" she said, like it was a book title.

"Girllll... He's not a hero so please..." he opened door wearing apron, half folded sleeves. Hair strand was on his face.

"Oh you bring friend... I was wondering not you having friends?" his fake sweet accent. How he switched his personality so fast? I rolled my eyes and entrered in without any reaction.

"And you?" he stopped Alan.

"Ohh, hello sir I'm Alan... Your neighbor and Rose's best friend"

"Male friend? Rose you have male friends too?"

"Is it crime?"

"No, but you're not invited in my house" he shut the door on his face, I opened it back.

"Alan coming in... He's my friend you can't dismiss him" I spoke for him.

"just friends or more than that?"

"Not every relation is end up where your thinking start" he raised his brows.

"That's my girl... Only for dinner... He won't stay night here" he gave permission.

Arthur went in kitchen.

"Ohh my god his accent is so hot" Selena was hyping him.

"You're stupid...."

"Your dad attitude is Sus..." Alan had objection.

"exactly what I was saying..."

"Talked with your mother"

"she's deaf... When it's about Arthur... I'm so done with this daily routine"

"Not him having work to do?"

"he says he's a business man but I see he's just interfering into my business"

"Hmmm....I'll keep eye on him from now, don't worry okay" I nodded, his caring nature always comfort me.

We had dinner, Alan went to his house. I locked myself with Selena in my room.

"why we're hiding like this?"

"No but... Do not open the door please... If you want water there's bottle and bathroom is here... I took some chips In case you're hungry... But do not open the door"

"Rose, if you facing some issues tell me..."

"that's exact problem... My issues are unexplainable... I can't... He's so smart"

"Okay relax... I won't open the door okay"

That Night, I couldn't sleep properly, my eyes were set on door, again and again I checked door locked. Once, I saw door was opened, don't know how but I went in sleep paralysis, I was moving my eyes around room saw him sitting in corner of my bed. Holding a sharp knife in his hand.

"Hello sweet heart..." I was struggling, my body was sweating but failed to move my body, he hovered me.

" What happened darling? Why don't you hear me huh?? This night could be more beautiful but you choose it..." he stabbed the knife into my chest.

I screamed, and fell off my bed. Selena woke up, she checked me. I was crying like a kid, Arthur was on door, he was banging my door.

" Don't.. Don't open the door... Don't please... "Selena gave me water.

" Shhhh you must had a bad dream relax... Come on everything is fine darling relax "

I hidden my face into her chest. She caressed my hairs.

Next Day, I woke up Arthur was sitting on my bed's corner, I got up.

"Relax... Selena was getting late so she left earlier" he explained.

"Get out of my room right now"

"fine, what you want for breakfast?"

"Poison"

"Unfortunately it's not available here... But if you insist I can buy for you..."

"I'm home" My mother's voice, I rushed down like I just freed from a prison.

"Hey sweetie, you okay?" she asked.

"Hmmm... Mom promise you won't left me alone again"

"Awww my baby girl... Okay I won't left you alone.... Arthur I'm hungry have you cooked something?"

"No, but I'm going tell me what you want?"

"First, you come in room" she called him with finger. Arthur followed her, he glimpsed at me when he closed the door. My head was aching, last night dream was horrible, still thinking was dream or reality?

It was hard time for me when it was beginning of my mother's Living relationship started cause I wasn't ready mentally and people thought Arthur was my sugar Daddy, No matter how much you ignore such taunts but people will pinch you with it.

I returned home, I was tired, my exams were going. Don't know what was on earth took my mother to open the door, she was late.

"Hey... Hi" she was panting, she said while managing her bra strip.

"Mom, give me keys when you planned fun time with your boyfriend" I was rude.

"Rose, behave... I was cleaning bathroom... What's this behavior?"

"huh... Good excuse mom... But I'm not a child, I'm hungry get me food... I'm coming"

I went up, washed my hands and face. I received a text message from Arthur.

Hey lil jerk... Do you want chocolates?

I was surprised, I texted him *NO* I went down mom was readying table I hugged her from behind.

"I'm sorry I was harsh.... Actually my exams are pain in my ass"

"Rose, mind your language... What will Arthur think?"

"Nothing I don't care what he's thinking, you matter for me"

"Darling soon we're going to marry... You need to accept him"

"Fine I will mom... Mom I'm going for group study so I'll stay at Selena's house tonight" I informed.

"Got ya... Have fun" she was a cool mother.

TWO

WHO KILLED MY MOTHER?

I

spent a night at Selena's house, didn't know, after that night my life going to be altered forever. Life is up and down but what if life is all about DOWN only?

I received Arthur's call, who called me more than 10 times already.

"Yes" with a lazy attitude.

"Where are you?"

"Not your problem..."

"Rose I'm coming to pick you"

"No... What the? I told mom... Ask her"

"I'm talking with you... Come home fast or I'm coming there"

"what the... Why are you making my life hell?"

"Your mom calling you... She's ill"

"What happened?"

He cut the call, I hate him button of my heart. I departed for home.

"Open the door" I banged my hand on it.

He opened the door with a straight face, I entered in pushed him aside.

"Mom..." I inspected her room, but she wasn't there.

"where's mom?"

"She's out..."

"you lied?"

"you didn't left any choice"

"Fuc... Where's mom?"

"as I said she's out..." he released a smile.

"You... Lying? You lying..." I shouted at him.

"Low your voice, you're creating a scene"

"I'll create for sure.." I moved towards the door, he caught me by my waist, his long hands crushing my ribs, I was shaking my legs in the air, hitting his hand, he covered my mouth with one hand.

"Leeevvehhhh" I murmured.

"if you behave... You won't end up like your mother, Rose... do you want to end up like her?" his words entered like lava in my ears, I trembled with my all strength. I bitten his finger, he removed his palm from my mouth.

"You bastardddd... What you did with her..? Helpppp... Somebody help Meeee" I was crying but no one heard me, he sat me on the chair, tied me with rope, and taped my mouth.

Hours later, I got totally dehydrated. My vision got blurred, he came with a glass of water untapped my mouth, I spit on him, he wiped. Fisted, don't know how much anger he was holding with that fist. He smiled, viciously.

"I decided to have some mercy on you but I think you deserve to die thirsty..." he jetted glass water in front of my eyes.

"Meet ya tomorrow... Good night" he tapped my mouth again and left me there alone on chair.

I was dying because of thirst. I went unconscious. Until he sprayed water on my face, I came to my senses.

"Morning, if you ready to behave... We make a deal... A good deal" he sat on chair like a king.

"What you did with my mother?"

"Nothing, she was out"

"where's she now? Call her"

"I called her but her cell phone is dead"

"why you tied me here?"

"you made me do... Who told you shouting like mad?"

"you imprisoned me in my house and you want me to be silent?" he tweaked his forehead.

"You're so stupid... I don't understand why you afraid of me so much? You always portrayed me like a criminal... Like I'm a serial Killer"

"who knows? I'm sure about it"

"woahhh.... What kind of serial killer?"

"who killed women and ate up their properties" he laughed his ass out.

"Come on Rose you never disappoint me whenever you crack joke... Am I look like a serial killer? How? How does your Lil brain work like this?"

"Your acts says all"

"Cooking for his family, buying gifts for you is a sign of a serial killer near you?"

"Yes, it is... You're a psychopath"

"decide first what I'm..."

"Devil"

"You keep changing dear... Nah choose one"

"fine.... Lucifer"

"He's hot" he winked transparently.

"I'm hungry... I'm thirstyyyyy" I screamed with all energy I had.

"Hmmm... Let's make a deal then you'll obey my every order, or I won't think twice before taping your mouth again"

I was helpless, I nodded with tears in my eyes. He got up from his place and placed the glass edge on my lip, I drank water.

"Rose, we can be good friends... If you behave like a good baby" I flared my nostrils. He untied my hands, I tried to run but he knocked me down.

"I knew that you'll try this stupid old trick... I was ready for..."

"Ahhhh my hand" I cried.

"I think you don't understand my language..." he sat me on chair.

"Fine... Fine I'll do whatever you say... I promise... I promise" I pleaded.

"I can't hear, I'm sorry..."

"Daddy.... I'm sorry... Forgive me for I have sinned" I bowed my head. He smiled.

"Good girl... That's my girl..."

He locked me in my room, seized my phone and freedom too. I was roaming in room like a mental patient. My anxiety was at its peak.

"Open the door... Open the door please" he opened it.

"what now?"

"At least remain this door open for me... It's suffocating"

"Why should I trust you?"

"It's been two days I'm here, without trying to escape... And you still asking me?"

"You didn't escape cause your ankle was broken..."

"I... No... I did whatever you said"

"all? You sure?"

"Look, I'm worried for mom... Where's she?"

"I reported her missing complaint"

"How calmly you saying this she's your partner"

"is she?"

"I knew... I knew that... You weren't loyal with her"

"I was but she.... Leave it.... Food is ready come down..." I went down with him, he cooked chicken.

"I don't think it's time for feast..."

"You wanna keep fast... Cause your mother is missing? Is she deserve this?"

"I thought you loved her"

"No... I was never... She wasn't deserving tho"

"neither you...." I puffed, I agreed on Lunch with him unless I would die out of hunger.

We were silently having lunch, heard knock on the door, my ears stood up straight. But my feet were stuck with floor. He got up.

"Hmmm... Yes... Yes, correct... Yes she's inside..." He came in hall with some police officers, I stood straight, before I said something, he put the finger on his mouth, signed me to shut my mouth.

"Hello... Sir"

"You're Miss Mia Daughter" I nodded quickly.

"Sit down miss please" they sat front of me.

"Where you were, when your mother went out?"

"Last time I saw her here... In house, she was happy, I was happy... But don't know all sudden where she went? Everything was good, I went for studies at my friend's house and next day Mr Walker called me"

He shrunk his eyes when I called him Mr Walker, like seriously! He thought I'm gonna call him Daddy front of officers?

"Hmmm... Look miss Rose... Unfortunately we found her body near the lake" I was in deep shocked, I felt like landslided under my feet, wanted to pinch myself to awake from that bad dream, my mouth was opened, I was expressionless, I looked at Arthur, he was watching my pale face. I stood up,my legs were flattering Arthur caught my arm.

"Miss Rose, we're sorry..."

"Who?... Who! How? She was okay... She said we'll talk about our future plans... She was happy... Officers she was happyyyy" I screamed out of my lungs, Arthur held me into his arm. I hung on his hand totally. My cry was too loud.

"I think it's not right time, we'll call you later sir.." they left the house. I was crying on floor like someone stabbed a dagger in my chest and squeezing it.

"Mom... Mommmm...... Mom was happy... What happened to her?"

"Shhh.. Shhh everything will be alright... Shhhh... Rose look..." I was kicking him, but still he held me tightly.

"Mommmm... I want my mom back... Bring my mom back... You said you'll marry her... You promise her... You liar" I beaten his chest, he hugged me, was caressing my hairs softly. No idea when I fainted there into his embrace.

When I opened my eyes, I was on my bed, Arthur was sitting near bed on chair, was reading a book.

"You killed my mother..." I blamed him, he shut the book.

"It's your theory"

"it's truth... I'll report in police"

"Fine, as your wish... I don't even care... My lawyer will clear their doubt in one sitting"

"You think you own anything you want?"

"No, I earn them..."

"Why my mom?"

"I didn't kill her"

"You did... I know... You lied to me... Imprisoned me here..."

"Outside is danger"

"inside is hell"

"It's your perspective"

"It's fact... My friends will inform police how brutally you treated me"

"Rose... I never hit you, that was all your made up situations if there's marks on your body it's because of your own self..."

"You did that to me" he rubbed his forehead.

"What you want to eat for dinner?"

"Poison"

"Uhhhh... I think I need order a poison bottle online"

He walked out of my room.

Police visited our house once more and this time I didn't think twice before calling Arthur's name as my mother's murderer.

"Are you sure ma'am?" they asked.

"Yes, I'm sure he's my mother's killer"

"but he was the one who reported her missing complaint"

"On my demand... I insisted him to do so..."

"Ma'am we're cross checking everyone and... Yes first prime suspect was your father... I mean your mother's boyfriend, cause forensic report said it was a planned murder... But we couldn't find prove against him... We just suspecting him with others"

"others? Like who?"

"We need to talk with Mr Walker miss"

They skipped me, I followed them and hidden behind Arthur's room door wall.

"Mr Arthur... According to forensic... She had sex before someone throttled her"

"So you thinking it was me? Sir if we need sex we won't meet in middle of forest, near lake... We having bed in our room"

"we know many cases where lover killed her partner just because of jealousy or for her property"

"I'm having a good bank balance sir, and jealousy? Why don't you ask him who was there with him... I didn't knew that she was sexually active with someone else..."

"Hmmm... We suspecting her colleagues..."

"she was used to going on trip with them, but now I know what was reason behind those trips"

"you must be angry on her"

"sir as I said... I didn't knew that she was including with so many others..."

"Fine Mr Arthur better you stay in city until this case close"

"when we can receive the body?"

"In two days... We'll inform you..."

They went out, I was standing behind him to be fallen on him with my harsh words.

"Wow... Great... Such a hoe you are? You had sex with her and then choked her till she die"

"Look, I'm not interested to having sex with her or either choking her... But yes if you say we can try... Choke me Daddy..." He smirked in evil.

"how shame less you are? Your wife..."

"Girlfriend... Or you can say, just for say.... Now I know what was your mother was doing behind my back..."

"huh if you gave her attention she won't do that"

"as you don't knew her? You know everything, but fact is we both acting we don't know anything... Right Rose?"

"if you knew her character then why you choose her?"

"I didn't choose her...." He was staring my face, with his brown eyes which having dark lashes.

"You used her... You're such an ass hole"

"I want to clear you, what you thinking it was never like that... We hadn't ever coupling... It was our promise, we were practicing for being a good parent and couple... So I did... I took care of you and her both... I did whatever she demand for but her lust end up on her death only" Don't know but his words were stabbed right into my heart, may be because he was correct, truth is bitter and it's true.

I was speechless, don't know why my tongue was stunned to speak, I silently went in my room.

Days passed, He kept funeral for mother, just for show. I knew that he was never belongs to her.

"Where's your phone?" Selena asked.

"He seized my bag"

"Ohh... When you going to join school back?"

"No Idea... I'm imprison in my house... Under his surveillance."

"is he insane?"

"Yes... He's totally sane... You don't know how I'm living with him in same house"

"why don't he just go back?"

"He totally accomplished my house, claim I'm his family, police said not to leave the city that's why he has strong reason now..."

"What if... He...."

"I'm sure he's killer..."

"it's danger"

"I know... But people said stay there..."

"Hmmm... You're totally trap... They think he's your dad"

"he's not saviour... He's real devil"

"Man in mask.... Where's the investigation reach?"

"They doing their job... But no clue... No idea with whom she was... But still my heart says Arthur behind it"

"Wishing you good luck dear... Take care... Did Alan visit you?"

"No, Arthur don't allow anyone... To meet me expect officers" we had a small conversation that day.

I was laying in bed staring ceiling, my mother's memories were flashing in my eyes.

"Psss... Hey.... Rose...." I heard Alan's voice, I was shocked when I saw him in my balcony.

"What you doing here..?" I scurried.

" I heard he seized your phone"

"Yes..."

We sat on bed.

"I'm sorry... I couldn't help you... Very sorry Rose"

"Alan...." my tears fell off my lashes.

"Shhhh... He'll hear you Rose"

"Alan.... I'm... I miss her"

"we miss her too, she was a..... Your mother"

"I wish she will ever understand me...."

"I wish too.... I know you suffered a lot"

Arthur kicked the door, my heart beat dropped. I held my chest, his eyes were red.

"Rose.... You know I don't like uninvited guests... Specially boys in your room"

I stood up. Alan hidden behind me.

"You won't hurt him..."

"He should think about it before"

"He's going... Alan go... Go Alan..." I shouted at him.

He ran towards the balcony, before he escape Arthur caught him and hung in air, he was flattering leg.

"Ehhh... Leaveeee..."

"Arthur leave him" he glared.

"I.. I mean... Da...daddy... Please leave him..." I shook him. But his grip wasn't loose on Alan's neck.

"Leave him.... Let him go.... I'll obey your every order like a good girl... I promise I swear... I swear my mom" He landed him on floor, Alan was coughing out of his soul. I rubbed his back.

"Get out..." Arthur said, Alan ran down for his life to main door, he escaped from house.

Arthur's eyes matched with mine.

"be ready on sharp 10" I nodded, cause my nonsense replies won't stop him now.

Next, Morning at Sharp 10 I got ready and went down, I remembered I used to squabble with him and now I'm listening him like he's my real Daddy. Just because of stupid Alan.

"Are you ready?" I knocked on his door after waiting for an hour. He opened the door, I won't lie but whatever Arthur wears, it suits him like it was invented for him. My eyes were stuck on him.

"Now don't tell me, you lost into me" I shook my head.

"Why you... Call me on 10 when you weren't ready?"

"I just wanted you to feel exact thing I feel when I wait for you...."

"are we going out?" I asked.

"Hmmm... Smart... Yes..." I felt butterflies in my stomach as he held my hand in his hand gently. I wanted to snatched it back but don't know why my body doesn't heard me when it should be obedient.

I stepped out with him, I was wearing a pink frock with black boots, clipped hairs, my attire was cute. But I was never fond of pink, it was my mom who forced me to wear this girlish color. A car was parked on gate, driver was standing out, he opened door for me I sat in, Arthur sat next to me. We left, I saw Alan was watching us from his balcony.

"What will they gonna think?" I said in low.

"Nothing.... And if they have any opinion about us, they can say it on my face"

First time in my life I was agreed with his sentence. Mom was correct we can be rich or a working woman but at a point we all need a man in our life to make us feel safe. Where it's a Father, Brother or Your Better half you need one.

My hands were shivering, I rubbed my palm on my arms, the car was comfy zone, all sudden my anxiety hits more and my legs started shaking. I fisted on my lap. He noticed he put his palm on mine. Okay, but what was that, did I just felt current in my body? Yes It was a free current supply.

"Why you're nervous?"

"huh... No who?" I lied. I looked out from window of the car, Arthur let me peeped out, he was remained in same sitting position. Soon the car stopped front of a big house. With a garden front. He opened the door for me and forward his hand, no idea what he was planning but as always I had no other choice, I gave him hand and walked with him inside the house, it was having beautiful interior with brown and black shades on wall.

"This is my house... You always thinking I'm interested in your mother's property which is a small house, I just wanted to show you I have my own property and I'm not prying for your mother's one. Actually I wanted to show you my place as you hadn't visit here before"

I was scanning his luxury house, when he stood behind me, and hugged me softly, I was freezed. He was rubbing his palm on my arms.

"Relax... Soon we'll shift here.... Okay..." he whispered in his deep voice, my senses weren't working.

"What do you like to have?" I turned face to him, his face was this close to mine.

He stared my lips, I folded them inside the mouth, he cackled, he kissed my nose tip.

"Don't worry... I won't kiss you..." finally he gave me some space, I took a relief breath.

"LET me make you coffee..."

"Pas... Pasta...." First time I replied him, properly. He smiled.

"As your wish princess"

THREE

WHO ARE YOU DADDY?

We spent a whole day at his place, I was lost in my deep thoughts, he sat on chair next to mine.

"How was your day today?" I just gazed at him.

"was that good?"

"Hmmm..." I bowed my head.

"You changed.... I'm not used to your polite behavior" did he tease me?

"No.... I'm.... I don't know..."

"You want justice for your mother? We'll find him... Okay..."

"Why are you helping Me?"

"It's not your...."

"It's my business.... Tell me... Why are you tolerating me? Why are you still with me?"

"Do you want me to leave you alone?" Don't know why but I couldn't say *No*.

"Say? Should I leave you in mid? Would you handle this all alone?" I nodded in lil, my eyes were teary.

"I heard what you don't even speak.... Rose"

"No one, help anyone without any benefit"

" I have my profit with me.... Right here" he held my hand, his warm palms roasted my cold fingers.

"It's warm..." I said in low.

"Then stay Rose.... I promise I'll keep it warm..." I nabbed my hand.

"I still don't trust you? And why should I we're still strangers" I stood, he pulled my hand, I sat down.

"Rose.... Give me at least one chance... Try to know each other... Why don't you ever think about me for the once"

"first of all you giving me creepy vibes... You're a stranger who forcefully involved in our family, my mother is dead and I don't know what I'm doing here?"

"You feel safe here... You doing here what you should do... This place belongs to you... You know after your mother no one is after you, and that's why you living with me cause only I'm... Someone who matters to you, who's cares about you... Don't I?"

I was silent, he was on point, yes I felt safe with him protected, after mom's death no one was there for me, Arthur was only person who took my responsibility.

" But I still scare of you... "

" it's because you don't know about me.... Rose I never date your mother if you weren't her daughter...." I knew that his target was me from the first day.

"and you did it, cheap..."

"No, approaching you directly was a stupidity, since I saw you first time in a shop with your mother I fell for you, you were disturbed and your mother was in her own world, I felt what you were facing that time, and 70% people are facing same problem in their life, not just others or their bullies are reason behind their depression, their parents too..... "

"And why you choose me? Just because I was living with my characterless mother"

"No... No I'm not blaming her, cause she faced so many things in her life too, but she was the reason behind your hell life. When I was 10 my mother cheated my father and he killed her during their fight. I thought it was squabble but... When it was turned into a murder case... I couldn't had idea... I was too young and since then my uncle raised me, I study and work hard.... I wanted to show them I'm not like my parents, and I proved them... I earned this all. But when I saw you I saw myself in you, I was worried, what if one day you too.... " he paused.

" I'm sorry for your mother..... But for me... You'll be my mom's ex.... Don't tie any hope with me"

I got up from the place and went upstairs.

Next Day, I woke up in bed, I went down, servants were working in kitchen, hall everywhere.

"Is this special day today?" I asked a maid.

"Yes ma'am today is sir's birthday.... Guests will be arrive here soon" I thought he don't have any family, but he was having a huge family tree.

I was sitting in my room, a man in his 30s knocked on door.

"Yes come in..."

"ma'am... Sir send a phone for you... There's only his contact saved.... He said do not try to call someone else other than him.... And yes your stylist will be here any time, have breakfast and Co operate with her, she'll help you get for tonight party" he said it all.

"Listen.... How many guests are invited?"

" No idea madam, but it's a grand party..."

He left, I sat down, sighed. My anxiety hit me, I hate crowdy places.

Evening, The stylist helped me ready for party, she selected a black gown for me, and left my hairs open. Did a smokey makeup said it suits me. Sprayed a spicy perfume.

My legs were shivering, already the house was full with guests. I knew that the moment I stepped out everyone gonna freezed their vision on me. Not because I'm beautiful, but yes for judging me, or some will probably say I'm a whore. Arthur's decisions never get in my head.

I stepped out, as expected everyone was goggling at me. I was nervous as hell before Arthur tuck his arm into mine. I looked at him, birthday man himself walked down with me. First time in my life I felt special. Very special.

"Happy birthday Arthur" a woman in red slim dress wished him, she was holding a wine glass in her hand, God she was gorgeous.

"Thanks Georgia.... I wasn't expecting you here"

"But I was waiting for this day... Entire year"

"Well unfortunately my birthday comes once in a year...."

"BTW, I'm so sorry for your... Ex..." She gave me a vicious look.

"Meet my baby.... Rose..." he hugged me from side.

"Baby?? Not she's same girl...? I thought she's your step daughter"

"I'm sorry but do you think I'm father of a 15 years old daughter?"

"Noooo... You're still young..." she winked, seems like she was interested into Arthur but biggest question was why Arthur was interested into me when Woman like her was already in his life.

Arthur introduced me one by one with his family members and his office employees. I thought people would say, I netted him because he was rich. But people was comfortable and accept me as his Baby. Don't know in what way they accept me his Baby as a father or Daddy?

After party, I changed my clothes, I was combing my hair front of mirror, Arthur entered.

"Hope you enjoyed the party" He stood behind me, my head was reaching his shoulder.

"You were looking gorgeous tonight" he whispered, I closed my eyes. He smelled my hairs, while trailing down his palm on my arms. I was stunned. We end up facing each other, he brushed his nose on my face. I blinked.

"Sleepy?" I nodded. He kissed my cheek, don't know the more I hate him, more I liked his touch.

"Good night..."

"Georgia will stay with us here?"

"US???" He pressed the word.

I turned my eyes on left.

"Hushhh finally you consider us... As US.... Yes she'll stay here for some days"

"When she'll go?" I asked innocently.

"You don't like new people, right?" I was staring into his eyes.

"Hmmm... Don't know, but she says she has some work to do, later she'll go"

"Okay."

"I suggest you, Do not talk with her.... Stay in your room until I return" I nodded as an obedient baby.

"Can I... Can I save Selena's contact in my phone...? Please" I pleaded.

"Rose...."

"Only hers... Please... I'll be bore in this house alone... Please...."

"Fine... But no one other than her" I agreed.

"When I'm gonna join school?" I made another wish.

"Not now... Your mates will bully you.... Give exams next year"

He walked out, I didn't object cause he was correct this year was already wasted and after mom's death my mates will bully me more.

I installed my social media apps and logged into. Arthur told me not to add my friends numbers but I can contact them here. I was scrolling my phone screen I got a message from a stranger who sent me my mother's Death body picture and said if I wanted to know the culprit then I have to meet him exact on 3 afternoon. At same place. That was suspicious who inviting you on a murder spot, and being not a stupid girl of every single story I decided to sent the text to the police.

When Arthur return home, he saw police with me, he got worried.

"Is everything okay?"

"Sir, your daughter received a message from an unknown account and he called her to meet on murder spot..."they explained in short, he checked my phone, his stare was killing, I pretend I wasn't there.

"What you officers doing? Here someone texting her to meet him at murder spot, next he'll stalk her and kill her too.... What you guys doing with your job? Don't have any single clue...?"

"Sir, we trying our best, we checked her call records her social media accounts but seems like the person was a master killer he don't left any clue behind"

"Of course he won't left his foot prints for you to follow him you have to find them and it's your job.. It's your responsibility to find him soon... I can't take risk for Rose..." His tone was harsh and loud. I hadn't seen him this much angry before.

"We...."

"LET me talk with your seniors... I think this case is not under your control ...."

"Fine whatever you want, we're doing our jobs and we had other cases too... It's your responsibility too protect your family too..." they dispatched the destination. Georgia was drinking juice on counter, she was smiling at my stupidity think so.

"Your baby is bomb.... She's creating problems in your path" Arthur glared, I gulped he caught me with my arm and went upstairs while towing me with himself, he pushed me, I fell on floor.

"I'm sorry...." I said in heavy voice.

"Didn't I warn you....?"

"I thought if I...."

"Rose what you thought? Social media is danger for you, anybody can contact you... Anybody can locate you... And I can't be here 24/ 7....just to babysitting you" he never talked like this to me, I was who always shouting on him. I think I crossed his patience line.

"I'm Sorry... Daddy...." may be this is how his temper will cool down. But his forehead muscles still on point.

"Give me your phone..."

"Dad.... Daddy... Please...."

"I said give it to me.... Can't you hear me...?" his thunderstorm voice shuddered my heart.

I gave him my mobile phone, he slammed door. I was sad. But It was my mistake I couldn't blame him, but who knows he texted me? Wait... What?

Days Passed, Arthur stayed at home more than office. Now mom's case transfer to crime branch. And Georgia was still at home, Arthur was upset with me, he don't talked, don't eat with me, ignoring me all the time like I did a sin. And the bitchy Georgia was waiting for that moment for her life.

"I think you should dropped her home back... She's just creating more problems" she spoke, I was listening them from wall behind.

"Mind your business Georgia and if you done with your work you can go"

"this is rude... Arthur this is how you behave with your uncle's daughter?"

"I'm polite... I'm busy excuse me" she stopped him, pulled his arm.

"Look at me... Look into my eyes.... Don't you see love for you? My love for you?"

"what is love? I don't know.... I don't believe in this four letter word"

"Arthur come on... You can bear her stupid acts but not my sincere presence?"

"your presence is pain in my ass...."

"why you hating me? Huh... What I did?"

"Georgia I'm happy alone here, don't make my life hell... Better you go back home.."

"this is home... You're my home... I want your embrace around me.... I feel safe between them" she kissed his cheek, they were too close, I wondering why Arthur wasn't stopping her, was he enjoying that? Huh, why not once a man always a man... He must be lost into her deep hot breath... She had experienced of men and how to exploit them.

"Arthur I can give you everything you demand for.... I can fulfill your every wish you ever dream for..." she slided her hand down to chest and unbutton his shirt, I turned myself. That was... Something I couldn't take. I was boiling inside. I fisted, my body was trembling, my anger level was on its peak, but unfortunately I couldn't kick in her ass right.

I was sitting in my room, writing my diary but my tears were fading my writing. I stopped pen and head down. I was crying, I cried and cried, until my inner grief fully drained out.

I heard door noise, I wiped my tears, Arthur put the plate on table, I hadn't my dinner yet.

"Finish it fast..." he ordered. My head was down. When he observed my diary page. He towed the chair, sat down.

"Hey...Rose... Look at me... Rose..." he pulled my chin up. My swelled eyes says it all.

"you were crying?" he huffed.

"what happened now? You missing your mom?" I didn't answered, he kept asking me but I zipped my mouth already.

"Rose why you don't speak.... This is what makes me more mad at you..."

"You change..." only two words I spoke.

"what? What you said?"

"you have changed...."

"What?? Look who's talking... Who made me change myself just because of her stupid activities and now you blaming me?"

"It's not about phone...."

"then what?"

"Your behavior... You always scolding me, ignoring me, glaring me, staring me, only thing is left beating me..." he was this close to laughed out his ass, but he maintained.

"No I was always same"

"No you were not..... You were...." I paused.

"I was... What?"

"I don't know.... Go to your Georgia.... She must waiting for you..." he bitten lower lip.

"Hmmm correct why I'm passing my time here? Finish meal and sleep...." He stood up, he took a step forward, I pulled him with his hand. He bend lil, I up my head but shit he's still tall for me... What an embarrassment... Such a shame, most inelegant moment of my life. I maintained distance. I couldn't made eye contact with him, my legs flattering, I was taking back step, looking down. I saw Arthur stepped towards me, my heart beat increased. He held my hand softly, pulled my chin up. I managed looking at door.

"Rose... Look at me...." I managed to look at his face, I was literally red.

"Were you trying to...."

"No.... I... My ankle... It's hurting... I was taking support"

"It's most ugliest excuse I have ever heard"

I bitten my lip. He smiled finally. He closer his face to mine, I was shaking inside, he put my hands on his shoulders and pulled me closer with my waist. I was looking right into his eyes. He tilted head, closer his mouth, I closed my eyes, he pressed his lips on mine. I felt butterflies in my belly before he started kissing me, he gentle kissed my upper lip then lower one, I followed his movements, he tightened his grip on me, the more he tightened his grip the more I feel good, I wrapped my arms around his neck. We were lost, that was my first kiss and I was glad that Arthur was my first kiss, indeed he was best. We kissed for minutes, I broke the kiss. I was blushing so bad. My eyelids were shedded. He kissed my cheek tight.

"You don't know, how long I wait for this moment...?" I blushed more.

"Now you trust me.... Right?" I looked at his face.

"No...." he picked me bride style.

"I don't care.... Only thing I know you're mine.... Just mine." I was hating his Dominant nature, but that day I fell for him once more. I placed my cheek on his chest.

"You.... You won't left Me?" I asked with puppy eyes.

"No... Never love...." he kissed my forehead.

The night he slept on my bed, shedding me into his embrace, I hidden my face in his chest, fell into slumber. That was my most Beautiful night of my life, cause I felt affection, care, love for me first time and realized why people do love? want someone in their life, that one person.

After that night things gets lil better, I started more smiling, Arthur everyday bought me gifts, I wasn't a kid but my inner child want that, he took care of my every little thing. Often he slept in my room and I had no objection on, cause he was my favorite now.

"Hey Sweetie... Are you free?" Georgia, peeped in my room.

"No..." she came in.

"Did Arthur said, not to talk with me....?"

"No...."

"I know he said.... Cause he afraid... Won't I unwrapped his real face front of you" Those bitchy eyes.

"What?"

"Did he told you, his father shot his mother....?"

"Yes"

"Oh, you're cool.... But do you know Arthur was in mental hospital for 5 years... I supported him, I made him a human... After his mother death he turned all savage, he's just like his father, over possessive, insane and ruthless.... Who knows he killed your...."I changed my expressions.

" No look... I heard she was cheating on him? As he said, but who knows she wasn't cheating him, actually Arthur was interested into you since first day... I was too shock when I heard he's dating a woman older than him... "

" Older?" I was shocked.

"Ohh sweety don't tell me, he lied you? Your mom was 30 right.... And Arthur just complete his 28th year...." I was in deep thoughts.

"I'm so sorry but it's his nature... He lied... He want what he wish... No matter what... I know he's attractive... That's why I'm here too even I know his real face instead, you haven't saw his sane phase what I experienced .... He's a good actor... Don't let you know what he's thinking inside... "her words accomplished my head, my all perspective changed for Arthur.

I was processing from that new attack, his manager knocked on my door, my heart beat dropped.

"what??" I was scared.

"I'm sorry ma'am.... Sir is calling you... It's urgent"

"what emergency?" She asked.

"Not your business ma'am... Miss Rose please fast it's urgent..." I took my hand bag and departed with him, entire way in car Georgia's words roaming in my head, that causing me head ache. I held my head, Car stopped front of a hospital. I got worried, I boarded down I thought something wrong with Arthur, but he was waiting for me outside there. I rushed towards him, he spreaded his arms, I hugged him tightly, after seeing him okay I forget all things

Georgia said about him, it was truth Arthur was most charming man alive for me.

"Hey, you okay?"

"Hmmm... I'm okay... What happened?"

"Selena... She's serious" one more attack.

"What? All sudden? Where's she?"

"she's in ICU... Police said she called them before she met accident, she said she knew something about killer..."

"Mom's killer?" he nodded.

"Who?" I asked.

"before she said his name.... She got inaudible"

I fisted my hair, he rubbed my back.

"What Doctors says?"

"They can't give guarantee... Pray for her..." his tone was polite.

I went inside, once had glimpse of my friend who was fighting for her life.

"Sir... Please come side..." he requested. Arthur went in corner with him. I shifted behind the wall, walls were my savior.

"Yes say...."

"Sir, You have an important meeting with Mr Coollen today..."

"I can't go.... Rose is alone here..."

"Sir but it's important"

"postpone date"

"Sir Mr Coollen insisting...."

"Fine you go... I'll stay with Rose..."

"Sir me?"

"Yes you, I trust you, you won't let our company down... Go... Have a safe trip" he bowed to him.

I thought, Arthur and his manager were hiding something but it was a business talk, how foolish I was, I came on my seat back before Arthur came.

"Rose... Lets go.."

"Where we going?"

"Having lunch... I booked a room at near hotel, don't worry we'll visit her tomorrow okay..." How could I don't trust person like him?

I held his finger, followed Daddy like obedient baby.

I was sitting in hotel room, Arthur checked in.

"I know it's hard time for you.... Because of me first your mother left you... And now your best friend" he said while undressing his coat.

"Selena must know him... Who can he?"

"No idea love.... Seriously.... May be that killer text her same message as he did to you... Or he's some serial killer" he shared his thoughts.

"who hates woman... Who cheating on their partners?" Arthur was unbuttoning his shirt he paused, he gazed me through mirror.

"Georgia.... That's why I told you not to talk with her...."

"You lied... You are not older than my mother?"

"Yes, she knew that... I lied to you, cause she said it to me..." he cleared my first doubt.

"You been in mental hospital for five years?"

He take off his shirt, I face the wall. He walked towards me, turned me, I was looking straight on his face, I swear. But he was damn hot. I can't denied.

FOUR
FORGIVE ME DADDY!

"Do you think I'm a mental person?" I nodded.

"You thinking I'm a serial killer who killing woman who cheating on their partner, cause my mother cheated on my father and that childhood trauma made me a serial killer? Rose don't you faced childhood trauma? Are you a serial killer?"

"but you were in mental...."

"yeah I was there... my uncle sent me there he wanted to declared me a mental patient and ate up my dad's property and so he did.... Any more questions?" I shook my head. He cup my face.

"Rose, I want you trust me just like I trust you.... Darling." his eyes saying something else, I clenched. He kissed my forehead.

"I'm sorry.... Daddy...." he smirked.

"Daddy, you won't let me down... Right?" he just smiled, I cupped his face and started kissing him, I wanted to clear the mess that I just made. He picked me with my back, I wrapped my legs around his waist. He laid down on bed while kissing me, I was over him, I was kissing him passionately, rubbing his bare chest with my palm, he turned me down, hovered me, he broke the kiss, his saliva was still on my lips, he was panting, I touched his face, my eyes were flashing his face, I down my lashes, he brushed my face with his sharp nose. I closed my eyes.

"I think you're tired... Sleep...." I opened my eyes, his face was this close to mine, I joined our heads. I was sobbing. He rubbed my arms.

"everything will be alright... Okay.... Don't worry Selena will recover soon" I agreed. He kissed my forehead. Laid next to me I hugged him, he cuddled, we slept.

Next Day, Arthur gave me good news, Selena Recovering fast and in no time she will be conscious. I took bath, changed my clothes, brushed my hairs, was ready at door to go.

"ready?" he asked while wearing his shoes.

"ummhmm..." I was so happy after hearing her recovery news.

"Let's go..." he held my hand we left for hospital.

When we arrived Hospital I saw Alan. He came there with his mother. I walked to him.

"Hi, Alan" he stood up.

"Hey.... I just heard about her...."

"any idea who can do this!"

"No Idea.... I swear... I don't know what she was doing these days? And why she was investigating your mother's case?"

"may be she know killer... I'm glad she's still alive"

"did she... Said something?"

"No before she said his name, she hit the car"

"So sad...." he hummed.

"Yes... But doctors says... She'll recover... Soon" Alan just nodded.

"Rose..." Arthur interrupted us, Alan excused himself.

"Yes..?"

"I have some work... Stay here with Selena's mother..." he noted me.

Evening, I was waiting on Arthur, he didn't returned yet. Selena opened up her eyes finally. On doctors permission Police interrogate her.

"Miss Selena... You were saying you have some information regarding Rose's mother?" she looked at me, I crossed my fingers, she nodded.

"Can you share that information with us?" she pointed her phone. They unlocked her phone with her help, they found pictures that astonished everyone in room, no was expecting this turn in the case. Their startled faces urged curiosity into me, I up my heels to peeped the pictures. And when I saw I was in extreme stupefaction. Like land slided under my feet. Police hurriedly escorted to arrest the real culprit. I sat down on chair next to bed, Selena held my hand, she was showing pity. Her parents was calming me.

Arthur entered in ICU, I collided with him, he hugged me back.

"Is everything okay?" he was worried.

"No... Nothing is okay.... No...." I started crying into his chest, he hugged my lil body.

Some truth are this bitter you don't wanted to even listen them, cause they filled this much bitterness in your life you forget what was the sweet taste like, don't know why people choosing path which end up on death or Shadyside. My mother gave me birth but since I born my life examine every day. I thought I will pass them all, but tough time breaks you down, that your knees kneel down and said, that's it, now enough.

And this is how criminals born that day. No one is bad since the day he born but people made them. Why they don't understand one day their shits will ate them up.

It been 2 Years, my mother's case closed, when Police reached out Alan's house to arrested him, he was committed suicide because of shame. His act was shameful that drown his parents into taint mud, I shifted with Arthur cause I don't wanted to face old neighbors more, Alan and Mom were in erroneous relationship that end up with their deaths. No body knows why Alan killed my mother? But police got some pictures of murder spot where clearly Alan and my Mother were coupling, and that was shameful. Selena recovered fully, and she complete her schooling after that incident. She too unawared who sent her those pictures but now everything was clear and silent.

I was living a good life with Arthur we decided, we'll marry after my eighteenth birthday. Yes, it was too early but not for Arthur and honestly, my inner woman wanted to marry him today. But Arthur wanted everything legal. May be he was so done with my alligations.

"Congratulations.... You scored full marks" He praised my report card.

"Yups... So what will you reward me?" I was excited.

"our wedding ring..." my jaw dropped.

"Seriously...??" I was super excited.

"Nope... Still for your eighteenth birthday there's six months left" he reminded me.

"Yes, I know..." I said sadly. He was working on his lap top.

"Arthur...." he was busy, I repeated. He gave me death stare.

"Daddy...." he shut the screen.

"What?"

"I observed you... I think you get bore of me"

"Ohh really? When I used you?"

"then use me..." I said shamelessly. He was surprised he smiled while blushing.

"You are.... I didn't expect you this horny..."

"I'm not... I mean... May be... Yesss..." I gave him puppy face.

"Now, you don't feel embarrassed?" he teased me.

"No... I mean.... No, my friends envy of me... They said... Your boy friend is hot..." I giggled like mad. He cackled. He pinched my cheeks.

"Arthur... Can I call you by your name? I know you're older than me but still...."

"Yes you can...." he gave me permission, I jumped on him, he catched me.

"This means your new friends are good?" Arthur admitted me in New school, where richy family kids can apply only. So for them sugar daddy, living and extra marital affairs were so common thing.

"Hmmm... I miss Selena" I said sadly.

"Why don't you call her here, for stay some days?"

"No... We're okay on video calls..." was I being possessive? Yes, I mean I don't wanted any one between Arthur and I. He was perfect.

"Okay now I have work to do... Go do your homework" I sat on his lap, and kept the laptop on mine.

"I'm giving you company...." he sniffed, he continued typing what he was typing was above my head, I was sleepy. I wanted his attention all the time, don't know he spend all day with me since he return from office but still it wasn't enough for me. I was always thinking won't some bitch came and took my place in his life. May be I was too obsessed with his scent that I can't share with any body else. But sometimes I felt like I'm imprisoned him now, and he's suffering because he said, yes. Or may be it was all my empty heads thoughts but still. His behavior and body language speaks to me like, I'm not his interest anymore. It's hurts.

I fell asleep on his lap, he laid me on bed.

Days Passed, and our routine was as same as before. Don't know but my inner voice was giving me hint to ask him what was the problem? There was something missing.

He returned from office, as usual. We sat on dinning table for dinner.

"Arthur..." he paid attention.

"am I... Am I boring?"

"No... You weren't...?"

"But... I'm boring now right?"

"What? Say it direct don't make net around" he came to the point.

"Don't know why but I'm feeling you have change... Arthur what's you hiding from me?"

"You don't know?"

"I swear I don't"

"Rose... What you hiding from me? First answer me" he crossed questioned.

"I... What?? I'm not hiding... Anything?" I scratched my neck. He was drinking soup.

"Fine discussion end here... You won't tell me so"

"What? What you want to hear?"

"You know what I'm asking Rose?" he glared. I gulped, my hands were shivering because of anxiety. I bowed my head.

"Rose say it right now... Or I won't trust you for rest of my life" he warned me last time. I gave up. My heart stopped. My hands were cold down. My body was sweating.

"why? Huh... Why?" He shouted, I shuddered.

"Cause I hate her...." I answered loudly. I burst into tears. I broke down.

"This much hate?" I was still crying.

"Yes... I hate her so much... She ruined my life totally... My life was hell.... She made me do that... She don't let any option for me... She was selfish... So I decided to be ruthless.... Cause I was her daughter after all" Arthur was disappointed.

"I tried my best to saved you from being a criminal and you...."

"cause my patience was end there... I can't hold that more... That was enough...." I screamed out of my lungs. He rushed towards me and held me, I was crying so much, he hugged me first, I hidden my face in his chest.

"I'm sorry.... I'm so sorry.... I'm really very sorry..... But she don't left any other choice for me.... Pleaseeeee...." I fisted his shirt, he kissed my head, relaxed me.

"okay fine we'll talk about it later... Okay... Don't worry.... I love you... I love you so much...." he cupped my swelled face, I was hiccuping.

"I love you too... Please don't left me... I'm not a criminal.... I'm not.... She made me monster...."

"I know... I know relax now... Clean your face... Okay... Shhhh shut up now..." he kissed me, I responded him. I hugged him, he hung me on him like a doll.

Next Morning, I woke up next to Arthur he was smiling, he tuck my strand behind my ear. I sat properly.

" feeling better? "I nodded.

" Now tell me.... What happened that day?" he demanded for, I don't even wanted to remember that terrible day but I wanted to shared with someone too and Arthur was best man.

"After I went Selena's house for studies, we went out for snacks, it was Evening. I saw Alan and Mom near the store, they were kissing, it was a shock for me, I couldn't believe that my friend and my mother he was too young, and mom not even left him? Her character was below anything in this world. I was hating her from bottom of my heart she never think about me, just her lust. I said

Selena to go home and said I forgot my book at home so I'll be back later... She agreed she went home, before they disappeared from my vision I followed them, they went on lake. I waited for them until they finished their pathetic coupling round, I recorded it all on my phone. When they leaving I encountered them.... They were shocked of course, but mom was still saying she wasn't wrong, she was cheating on you, I thought you forcefully came into our life but she was the one who was playing with both of us.... My patience answered me, don't know what happened with my mental health, I was so aggressive after seeing her with Alan... So I choked her with the table until she die.... "I finished, Arthur's face was blank, my eyes were wet. His silence was killing me inside.

"Arthur say something...." I requested.

"I'm wondering how can someone this good at acting..." I hidden my face with palm.

"Arthur pleaseeeee...."

"What the.... Girl entire time you were acting innocent but real culprit was you...." I turned sad.

"I'm so sorry....." I started crying, he giggled.

"Hey... Why you crying? What happened?"

"No... Nothing..." I sniffed.

"When I said, I'm going to call cops to arrest you..." I cried more, he cuddled me. He was laughing so bad.

"Hey sweet heart... Why you crying so? Huh... I love you so much and I won't let anyone snatched from me" I cleaned my nose in his shirt.

"I thought you'll... You'll leave me...."

"Huh.... If I wanted to left you... Then I would did that years ago... When I saw that videos In your phone...." I was blanked.

"Yes... I knew that you killed her since Start..." how calmly he said.

"Arthur?? How...?"

"I knew that she was cheating on me, but my aim was protecting you, I have decided I won't marry her I just wanted to make place in your heart. When I seized your phone I saw that video in your gallery, it was proof biggest proof, but I kept the copy and destroyed your phone same night, after that I reported in police. They had no clue from us we were saved"

"you were protecting me since Start even tho you knew... I..."

"Yes, I understand your situation, you are faced those all things since your childhood that stored anger with every year, and one day it gonna burst out... I'm not saying that was right but... How I explain you...?" I hugged him.

"don't explain me, just... Accept me as you saw me first time, I promise I'll be a good girl..." I promised.

"who said you're bad? You're still my good baby.... And I know it was all her bad luck and wrong time."

"Yes... I'm not a criminal... I swear I still regret that day of my life I don't know what happened to me... And I...." I again started trembling head to toe he calmed me.

"Relax girl... Relax.... Lets finish this chapter here" I nodded. He kissed me.

"Who? Who sent that message on my account?" Arthur raised his brows.

"Hawwww... And you shouted like it was my fault"

"didn't I told ya not to use any other apps? I was testing you... And you informed police, that exactly I wanted... At least you're not that dumb" I giggled.

"Later, unfortunately I had to add Selena in my plan just to forward police attention on her from you, so I sent her that video and she met an accident..." he shook his shoulder.

"You was behind that??" he was master planner.

"Yes, but we took care, we won't hit her she die and she survived..." I hit him.

"She is my only friend, thank God she's... Safe" I thanked God.

"That's why, I told ya stayed away from Alan since Start..."

"You knew that, mom was cheating you with him?" he nodded.

"But I don't like even girls around you... They fill trash in your head and starting quarreling with me..." I cupped his face.

"I promise I won't fight with you... Sorry Daddy" he smiled.

"Take care love.... I promise I'll give you best life..."

"You already giving me... Only thing mom did good in her life was, she introduced you with me...." he grabbed my waist.

"it was me who... Chased you till your home... Got it" I nodded.

"Well what's your next wish?" he asked.

"Ummm... I want to be 18 right now..." he raised his brows.

"why?"

"I want to be mother of a baby boy..." he joined our heads.

"your my life's happiness Rose, without you there's no color in my life..."

"and your favorite painting...." we lip locked with each other, he kicked on door and the door closed. Do I need to say, and we lived happy forever.....?

THE END

Printed by Libri Plureos GmbH in Hamburg,
Germany